W9-CCU-516

# JAMES REDFIELD *and* DEE LILLEGARD

# The Song of Celestine

*Illustrated by*
## Dean Morrissey

Little, Brown and Company
Boston  New York  Toronto  London

A restless boy named Celestine
felt unloved, unheard, unseen.
While wandering in the woods one day,
he found a path — but lost his way.

Celestine sat still as stone,
feeling cold, afraid, alone.
Looking down upon the ground,
he noticed leaves heaped in a mound.

Slowly, the air began to stir;
the leaves began to swirl and blur.
Taking on a new dimension,
they spelled two words: PAY ATTENTION!

Celestine's curiosity rose
as an army of ants marched past his toes.
He followed the ants in their steady crawl
until they reached a high rock wall.

*Pay attention, Celestine,*
said the voice of one unseen.
And Celestine saw a small door
where none, he thought, had been before.

Above the door, upon the rock —
above the door, which had no lock —
slowly appeared from first to last,
letters spelling TO THE PAST.

Celestine gave the door a push.
Then all at once he felt a *whoosh!*
as into a cavern he was swirled
and set in a strange, medieval world.

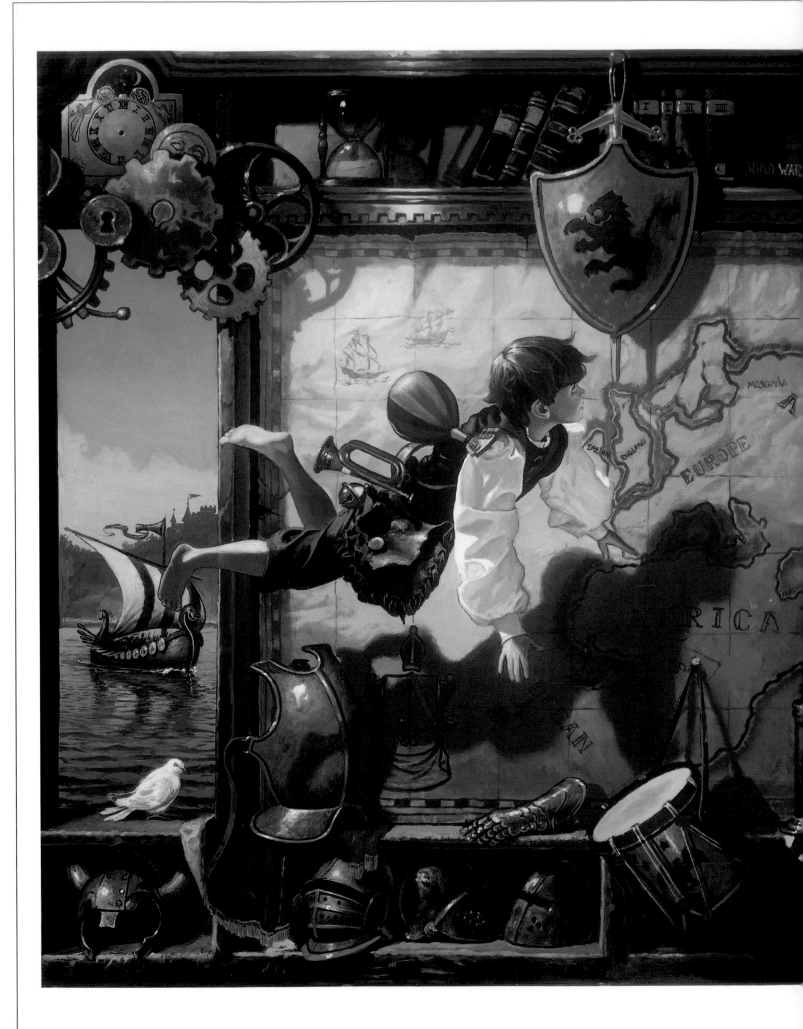

Celestine witnessed war after war
and people struggling for more and more.
He saw that the *past* was important *now*.
But why? he wondered. Why and how?

At last a light appeared ahead,
and roses blooming brilliant red.
Shimmering after summer showers,
their petals spelled the words TO FLOWERS.

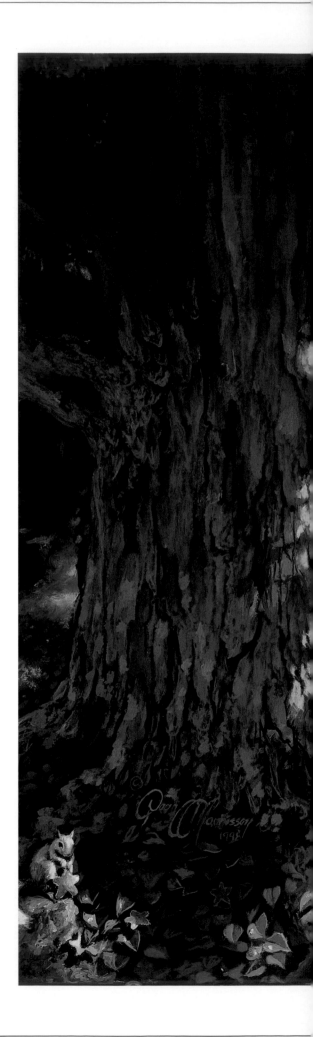

All around him flowers blazed;
their beauty left him breathless, dazed.
He felt himself begin to grow
and, deep within, begin to *glow*.

Celestine was filled, filled full
*with energy!*
Celestine was thrilled, thrilled through
*with energy!*

In the billowing clouds overhead,
letters appeared. TO FACES, they read.
Then close to Celestine a shadow formed,
and out of the shadow a warrior stormed.

The warrior, in an ominous tone,
claimed Celestine's energy for his own.
But I have to keep it! Celestine thought.
So in the fading light, they fought.

Celestine was thrown to his knees
under the shade of gnarled oak trees.
He glanced up and, there above,
beheld in the branches the word LOVE.

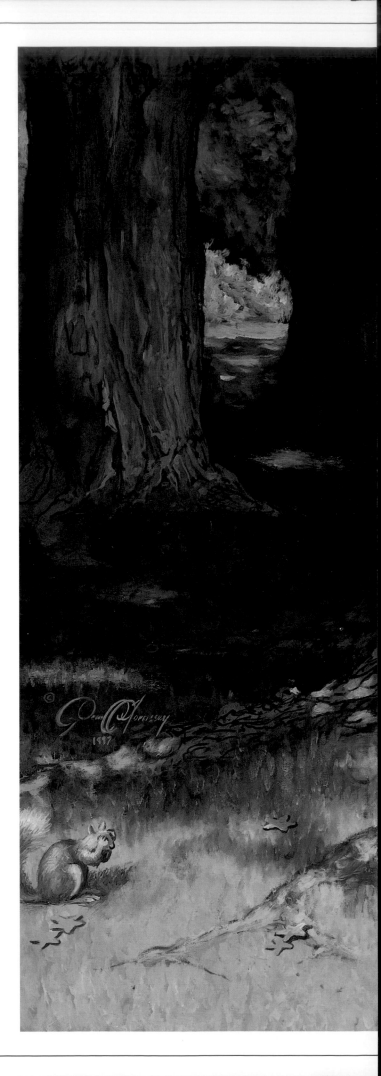

Celestine sensed a note of grace
as he gazed upon the warrior's face.
Then love began to conquer fear,
and he watched the warrior disappear.

Now came a crowd of butterflies,
dancing before his dazzled eyes.
Their colorful wings, softly spread,
spelled out letters. HOME, they said.

Celestine turned and saw a deer.
*Follow me…,* he seemed to hear.
He was still lost, but not afraid.
*Follow me….* And he obeyed.

Celestine followed on until
they reached a place upon a hill,
where, looking down, he saw a light—
*home!* Bright island in the night.

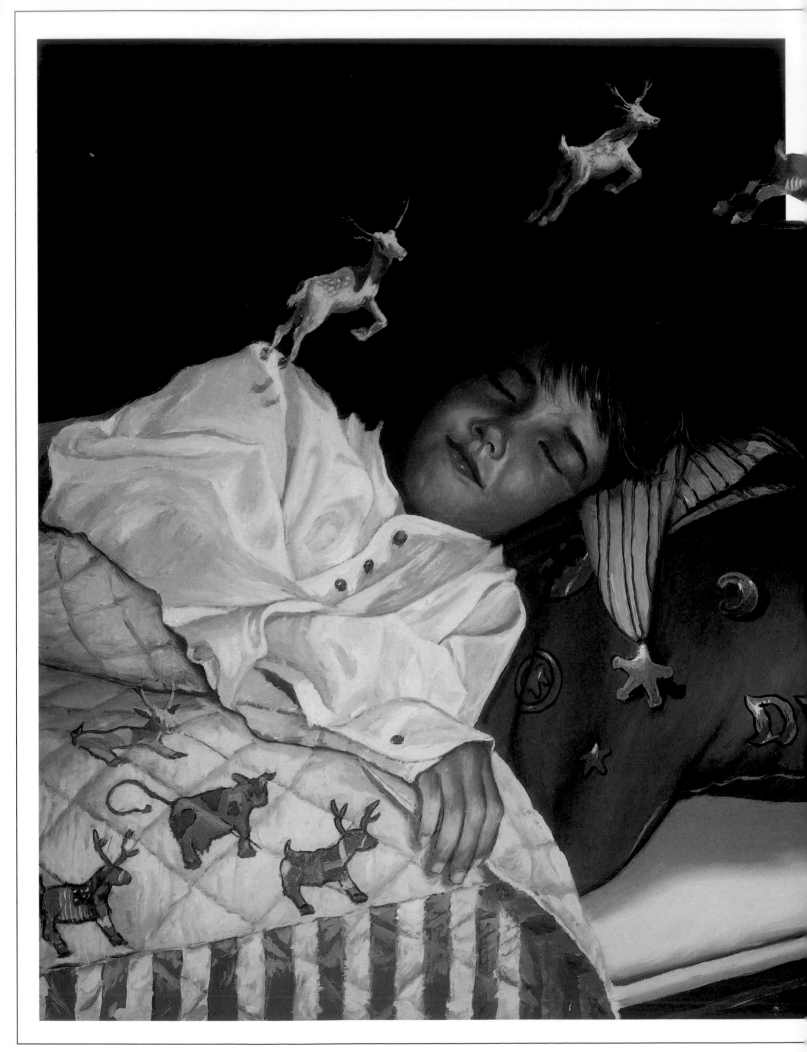

*Celestine, it's time for bed.*
Laying down his tired head,
he noticed on his pillow's seam
this embroidered word: DREAM.

Celestine dreamed of an echoing choir,
singing a note that rose higher and higher.
Then through the sky shot a brilliant flare.
A new word blazed; the word was SHARE.

Celestine woke and leaped from bed;
the messages raced through his tousled head.
*"Pay attention—now and to the past.*
*To flowers. To faces."* He was *home* at last.

And the choir sang in a single voice,
*"Love. Dream. Share. Rejoice!"*
Celestine knew from that wondrous day
that he would never lose his way.

And something else he had not known—
that he would never be alone.
Then he sang, too—as had been foreseen—
his song, the Song of Celestine.

To my trusted friend and agent, Kendra Marcus, who conceived the idea of a picture
book and believed in my ability to envision and create it
—D.L.

———— ◆ ————

Dedicated to Ian Morrissey
Special thanks to all the kids who came with me on this journey: David Morrissey,
Gary Morrissey Jr., Devin Newton, Amanda Morrissey, and Samantha Sawan
—D.M.

Copyright © 1998 by James Redfield, Dee Lillegard, and Dean Morrissey

All rights reserved. No part of this book may be reproduced in any form or by any electronic
or mechanical means, including information storage and retrieval systems, without permission
in writing from the publisher, except by a reviewer who may quote brief passages in a review.

First Edition

Library of Congress Cataloging-in-Publication Data

Redfield, James.
   The song of Celestine / James Redfield and Dee Lillegard ; illustrated by
Dean Morrissey. — 1st ed.
     p.    cm.
   Summary: A boy completes a quest by following the insights about life he
discovers around him.
   ISBN 0-316-73923-5
   [1. Conduct of life — Fiction.    2. Stories in rhyme.]  I. Lillegard, Dee.
II. Morrissey, Dean, ill.  III. Title.
PZ8.3.R246So   1998
[Fic] — dc21                        98-5874

10 9 8 7 6 5 4 3 2 1

MON-SP

D.L.TO: 527-1998

Published simultaneously in Canada by Little, Brown & Company (Canada) Limited

Printed in Spain

The paintings for this book were done in oil on canvas. The text was set in
Hadriano Light with Minister Light Italic. The display type is Goudy Handtooled.
Book design by Sheila Smallwood